PORTLAND: THOUGHTS AND PERSPECTIVES

Portland: Thoughts and perspectives, is a collection of writings about the place where I grew up. It is a place quite distinct from the rest of the county of Dorset in which it resides; a place of stone, wind, salt-sea air and separate history. The writings are not only about Portland, they are a reflection of my experiences, meditations on life and the realization of the cycle of life through the medium of my 'Portland' experience.

CONTENTS

A Statue for Portland

A statue carved from Portland's pure, white heart, stands admired on a sunny day atop the hill, as with fascination it draws the eyes of those who've made the climb. They also look upon the sight below and wonder how a view can stir such feelings from a scene so still; for land and sky in gentle harmony appear to bring tranquility to those who gaze a while before they go.

To feel the bliss of nature's calm so frees the mind, the better to appreciate the beauty of a monument that through an artist's eye was carved from Portland's influence, making for a special place and worth the climb.

A two-fold theme entwines within the statue, its dual appeal inspired by the flow of time; a place where passion, work and pain have left their trace, as shown here in industry - for quarrying and fishing lend their image to the island's space.

And so a circle comes full round with Portland's personality repeated in the nurtured stone, which blossoming has added to the island's grace.

A Sea View

A light-blue sky that occupies the top of everything with its apparent emptiness, floats on top of the deeper blue of the sea below, supported by a whisper. The sea seems troubled by eternal movement. It waves and churns as though in a permanent state of excitement.

The lighthouse stands before me in its red and white uniform - it looks like a sentry that's protecting the land from the sea. Its intense solidity contrasts almost painfully with the breathy spray of air and water behind it. Boy, that lighthouse looks solid! I think its mass would seem frightening if you touched it.

Hard, jagged rocks stand up out of the water. They, along with the lighthouse, make me marvel at nature's spectrum. How can it produce something as phantom-like as air as well as that impenetrable rock?

A large lump of metal weighing many tons floats across my view. It travels through the thin, invisible atmosphere supported by two whirling, narrow blades of flexible carbon. Some children, who are with their parents, shout and point at the helicopter as it rapidly moves along, its graceful progress contrasting with the sound of its continual growling.

This place they call Portland Bill now holds more mystery for me than it did when I was a child. In those days I wanted to get away from it as quickly as possible, so that I could return home to Verne Common, where I could run around with my pals. Outings with parents never had the same appeal as playing with your friends.

I draw closer to the area where the sea is attacking the land and listen to it ranting on the rocks below. Whoever said that Portland Bill was a peaceful place?

A Raft Of Hope

The rooftops of Portland echo to the sounds of our predecessors' dreams. The eternal cry has shrieked its message of existence since long before the advent of man's mechanical screams. And yet the knowing of this ancient sound, which in itself is history rebounding through the now, becomes rejected in the new regime.

A single seagull pays the price of its simplicity - its life squeezed out deliberately upon the tarmac cul-de-sac. The complexity that now prevails revealed its selfish anger when the swooping bird skimmed low - a protective and maternal move, yet irritating to a man whose anger has nowhere else to go.

Evolution's presence now lies broken in the road, its agony discarded amid the wrappings of a chocolate bar. One white and graceful wing waves to and fro, directed by the breeze that previously realised its part by acting as the pedestal of nature's art.

"So what? A gull is dead. There's thousands more," the young man said, while racing off to bigger things, he's satisfied his need to know the threat has been removed - for didn't neighbours say the gull had swooped before?

Reflection later in the day reveals the truth of anger's birth, as returning home the young man sees the place where grace still lies distorted. The reason why the seagull had to die is understood, as man and wife again retreat into a womb where seeds of separation bloom, fertilised by selfish loam and watered by desire.

The reflection of an attitude is noted by eternity and kept within a chain of circumstance. One car, one bird - the notion seems absurd, it will not change the course of history. But multiplied a billion times throughout a century and who can tell what price is to be paid?

A glaring sun beats down upon a newly blistered road where the balance line of nature stands revealed. We gamble at our peril with the selfish dice of greed, for if we lose the game we too in time will bleed.

But on Portland's hollowed shell we still have room to breathe and in many places nature still prevails. The thrill of hearing seagulls cry upon this raft of hope uplifts the heart where roaring traffic fails. To grant the birds a place to sing will to Portland fortune bring, as much as any fame where stone was carved; for any influence that helps to turn the selfish tide will in future's memory abide.

Portland's Trinity (A song for Portland)

Oh spur that holds the Channel's flow let independence mark. Tradition and a way of life ignites an island's spark, which gives birth to a flame of love and strength and unity. This place we know as Portland has championed all three.

That love is shown we need not doubt - take witness from the sky.

To save a life in jeopardy the selfless pilots fly. The coastguard ever looking out for threat of danger near, must lead the hearts endeavour to hold all mortals dear.

That strength be known is simply shown - observe the quarry's face. The pride of London city was drawn forth out of this place by hands that with both strength and skill extracted Portland's heart and passed it on to others, its spirit to impart.

United by their history the character behold of Portland folk whose ancestry is known through stories told. This placing of the heart through seeing meaning from the past ensures a kindred spirit that throughout time will last.

Anonymity

A hundred years to count the time - the clock in Easton Square looks down upon the ordered scene of people who show care. The heart's reflection all around we feel the need to mark by time's illusion born of thought, dividing light and dark.

A village life prevails the Square where people leave a trace; Everyone knows who goes where - the date, the time, the place. Anonymous does not reign long, succeeded by a king whose ruling heals the wounds endured through lonely suffering.

For friendship warms the shielded square as if by Royal decree, it's blessing comes to those who've lost their anonymity.

Braving the Storm

(Based on the final moments of Henry Gosling, who was a member of the crew aboard the 'Colville' - a West Indiaman, which sank off the Chesil Bank in 1824 with all hands lost, of which seventeen were buried on Portland.)

We had rounded the Bill of Portland when grey skies and an increasing swell gave us late warning of the fast-approaching storm, as it easily raised the ship high then dropped her down to the dirge of an increasing wind. Being several miles out into Lyme Bay and with no time to attempt to put into port, we were forced to ride out the bad weather as best we could.

We lowered the sails and stood on the deck of the heaving vessel, where we gazed towards the rising tumult, which by the look of it seemed set to test to the limits our will to survive. Evidence of our future misery was revealing itself through the expansion of huge, black clouds, whose towering scale alone was enough to tempt panic into the heart of even the most experienced sailor. Before long, the arena of our nightmare displayed a sinister quality through the lowering of the sun's radiance to the level of twilight. Like a condemned man watching the construction of gallows before his prison window, the darkening sky had brought us to the point where foreboding ruled us, as it began to form shapes out of our anxiety. Such was the threat from the gathering maelstrom that it was too late to set our suffering aside until its physical manifestation took hold, for fear's conviction had already started the gnawing despair that gripped the guts of every man aboard.

The vessel was turned around to face into the increasing swell, which was gradually forcing us inland towards Chesil Beach. Soon, the added trepidation brought about by near total darkness would probe at the weakness in the mental fabric of each member of the crew. Once the desire to resist the probing gave way, the vicious circle of doubt would begin in earnest. God help the man who lost control when his world was being thrown and smashed by a billion tons of water, for that man's need would be greater than any other's.

The ship continued to rise and fall at an ever-increasing angle, as she rode the waves, every now and then her decks becoming awash when she was caught broadside by a lurching shoulder of water. The pelting rain was a flood by the time Daniel Tate staggered over to me with a bottle in his hand, his long hair hanging in sodden rat's tails at the sides of his face. Swaying beside me, he reached out and drunkenly pulled me to him.

"Ah Henry!" he cried into my face, his voice barely audible above the crashing of the waves against the hull and the gusting wind. "This is going to be a bad one. I'm losing my faith in our chances with this one."

I looked down at his wrinkly countenance and into the drunken eyes, where the moistened pupils reflected a gleam of terror. The distraction of his display of hopelessness angered me so that I wrenched his hands away and pushed him back, my action causing him to fall over, his bottle flying from his hand and rolling off and away across the tilting deck, where it smashed against a bulkhead. I immediately regretted my loss of temper when my own feelings of dread returned, crushing my spirit, yet at the same time allowing a surge of sympathy for the plight of Daniel - a regular drunkard who had now lost his only chance of numbing what might be his final agony.

All thoughts of Daniel dissolved as I turned my gaze back to the bow of the ship, which seemed to be at a new angle to the oncoming, mountainous waves. The foam and spray that issued forth from these thirty foot giants was being regularly illuminated by flickering lightning, each flash adding to my desperation, as the outline of the storm's gargantuan features became horribly apparent, having been momentarily hidden by the darkness.

Suddenly, I realised a change had taken place that would likely seal our fate and which left my jaw fallen open and my body tingling with horror; for the ship had now turned on her axis and was broadside on to the towering waves - a position that would almost certainly result in our destruction and which would be well nigh impossible to correct.

Daniel was still lying upon the deck, where he would occasionally reach out to other members of the crew who were scrambling past, some with wooden objects in their hands, which they intended to use as floats once the inevitable had happened and they found themselves flung into the sea. Two or three desperate souls were emptying small barrels and kegs of their contents, while others had hold of lockers and chests that they'd brought up from below decks. I could hardly bring myself to action - the storm having mesmerised me in the way that a snake does to a mouse.

However, the urge to survive being great, I too found myself struggling along the rolling deck, towards a hatch that would allow me below and into the hold, where many tons of cargo were stacked, including barrels of rum and spices. Once there, I chanced upon a barrel that was empty, but before returning up on to the deck with it, I found myself suddenly affected by an understanding that the next few moments would be my last, and that any preparation to aid escape was futile and useless.

My next thought was to tear a piece from my shirt and to write my name upon the remnant. I felt that if I was unable to save myself, I was still in a position to make my last act in this life one that would be of use to my beloved family. Tying the material around my neck would allow a means of identity, should my body be washed ashore. Having satisfied myself that the cloth was tied secure, and with the blessing of hope being not quite dead within me, I grasped the barrel and ventured back up to a scene that made my blood run cold.

The ship was listing horribly and in such a way that the tops of the waves were falling quite freely onto the deck. As if by design, a flash of lightning forced me to witness death's final approach, as I realised that our starboard side was facing down into the trough of the next wave and that the vessel was already beginning to sink. As I glanced up at the incoming wave, I knew that my view of the world above the surface of the water would be my last. I threw the barrel aside, dropped to my knees, placed my hands together as though in prayer, and stared into the cathedral of life that is the sea - then waited for that place to swallow me.

Church Ope Cove

Anonymous to many, you lie as a hidden alcove of delight at the feet of maternal cliffs that shield you from the might of wind and rain; a haven, guarded by an ancient fortress, which presence proves history's regard for your mysterious domain.

To land a hoard in secret on your shore is what you're for - you tempt my mind with notions of the past. Did a light shine out upon a darkened sea and beckon in the bounty from a ship of fortune, or are these ghosts a dream ignited in my mind by your entrancing flame? No registries of such events remain - the truth entombed with those who might have played a dangerous game, which cost them dear.

But now, your unexpected prize is known by eyes that buy a place upon your hill, and feed upon your tranquil grace from wooden huts where sun and sea together forge the mystery of joy's elusive chemistry, so seldom found in noise and faster pace.

To walk atop the craggy hill, or just to sit and lose the day by gazing out across the way, rewards with patience those who cannot wait. Their stormy haste to better all that is becomes a breeze when on your changeless scene they contemplate.

Green, blue, bright and still are words that seem applicable to you; the sunshine in my mind breaks through - released somehow in composition scribed by nature's hand. But should there come a day when a witness has to say that the crime of your destruction has been seen - that a grey and wasted place now lies where you used to lie, for the sake of selfish memory let that witness not be I.

Dreamer's Cottage

Our house, I'd like to mention, has changed its dimension since its birth in Easton Square more than a century ago. It's grown at the rear to the tune of one room and rearranged its innards to look more like a home. Originally a shop that retailed fags and pop, it even had a Co-op sign above its window frame in nineteen-twenty-two. A photo proves the point and hangs upon a wall inside, like a picture of a child whose face has grown and changed - the premises displays its youthful past.

Outside, and at the back, a small and private garden elevates above a patio where birds sit in an apple tree and peck at seed from feeders. All shapes and sizes gather here - it's like a social club, it seems as though they've nowhere else to go.

On summer days we sit in comfy chairs and gaze across the lawn, as flowers slowly rise behind a dry-stone wall - we too can rest in peace a while and carry on the dream that started oh so long ago.

EASTON

Easton village: comfort within the hard, cold surround of stone's barricade. Human frailty nurtured amongst scarred landscape where wind dictates winter's siege upon the elevated platform of an island's open vulnerability.

Easton Square: a small place, but with a voice that sings loud the chorus of Portland's melodic and varied song. The outer wildness here gives way to softer tones that play inside the gentle basin of Portland's centre, where even the ruling wind must slow and lessen its subtle friction on the land. Easton Square is the warm hearth of Portland's draughty living room.

MEMORIES OF PORTLAND HARBOUR

A gently undulating spectrum of colour floats in a small patch on the harbour's otherwise clear water surface. It has formed a barrier that keeps me from probing the life-ridden harbour floor, which is probably only five or six feet beneath my squinting gaze. However, through the refractive effect of the water, the distance to the soft, muddy bed appears, when I glance to the right of the floating patch of oil, to be considerably less than five or six feet. Now that I have placed my concentration away from the floating rainbow, a small portion of nature's aquatic abundance goes tantalisingly in and out of my focus with the movement of the sea's surface, which also has the effect of gently rocking the wooden jetty that is supporting my young body, as I lie face down on it with my head dangling over its shallow edge.

I turn my head to left and right, in order to help with the focusing problem, after a flash of silver catches my eye when a shoal of whitebait turns itself instantly around in one united movement, as though it were a single fish. The instantaneous shift of these little creatures fascinates me in a way that conjurors do when they appear to achieve the impossible. I wave my hand quickly just to see them flick round again, as they respond to my signal.

Eventually, I find an area of water that allows me to see with clarity to the bottom, where my eager eyes feast themselves on a small, black-shelled crab that's crawling sideways in what to me is a gruesome and insidious manner - my feelings towards the crab family being best described by such schoolboy adjectives as 'orrible. The crab continues to wander sideways into the blurred area of the underwater jungle, and as nothing else of immediate interest appears on the scene in order to entertain me - I get fed up and look elsewhere for excitement.

Having stood up from my prone position, I hitch up my shorts, adjust the 'S' belt around my waist and look across the water towards the two huge, floating Mulberry harbour blocks to the left of my vision, which seem somehow to compliment the heavy and threatening presence of the guided missile destroyer to my right, both of which are within two hundred yards of the jetty on which I am standing. The weather is slightly overcast, which seems to add to the sombre atmosphere generated by these two reminders of war. At least, that is the effect they have on my mind as I look back on my childhood memories, although I think at the time the presence of the Mulberry harbours and warships made Castletown beach an even more desirable place to visit.

The beach is a very small affair with perhaps only a dozen rowing boats and an equal number of fishermen's huts positioned across its width. Adjacent to it is the naval dockyard, which frustratingly for me I cannot enter, as I do not have a pass that will allow me in. However, I don't worry too much about this limitation because if I walk two hundred yards back down the road that leads through Castletown, I can turn right into the naval sailing centre, which also boasts a small beach, and what's even more exciting - a row of rusty, old pontoons that jut out into the sea for about seventy yards. From these pontoons my friends and I can leap into the shallow waters at will and fish for prawns and shrimps with our nets. Should we grow tired with that, we can decide to run a few yards across the beach and climb the outer ramparts of Portland Castle, or balance our way along the sewer pipe that becomes exposed at low tide, in order to try and catch what to me and most of my friends are particularly evil-looking crabs with our fishing lines. Whatever we do, we usually end up generally exhausting ourselves by running around in the heat of the sun and splashing about in the sea until it's time to go home. If I've made all this sound like an idyllic way for a child to spend their summer holidays, it's because in my opinion it was.

It was during this period in my life that I met a character who was known to us kids as Wilkie. He would have been in his sixties when I first came across him at Castletown beach, where he operated a small trawler, which he used to take parties of anglers on deep sea fishing expeditions. The deep sea in question was usually the Shambles Bank, which lies about three miles off Portland Bill and which was well known to have a fair-sized population of turbot gliding their flat bodies around on the sea bed. Wilkie also had a smaller boat that was moored alongside the wooden jetty, which was used for taking tourists around the harbour on sightseeing tours - a venture that I was to become personally involved with about a year or so later.

The first thing about Wilkie to strike my ten-year-old mind was that he seemed frightening. He must have been over six feet tall and heavily built with a face like that of a professional boxer. His weathered, wrinkly, brown skin, toothless mouth, greasy, cloth cap and flat nose (which I later found out he acquired in an accident and not in a boxing ring) in themselves only partially bothered me, but when they became combined with the raucous shouting that emanated from him whenever he chased me and my mates along the front of the fishermen's huts on his motorbike (which I remember happened on more than one occasion) I found myself shrieking in fear just like the others. There was something about Wilkie that made you think that he might just run you over. However, as far as I know he never hurt anyone and my memories of him are fond ones.

I became involved with Wilkie's harbour sightseeing trips about a year after I first met him. My mate, Robin, managed to persuade Wilkie's young assistant, who operated the sightseeing boat for Wilkie during the summer evenings, to let me sit alongside them on the boat while they waited for the visitors who occasionally turned up to look at the warships from the excellent vantage point of Castletown beach. When people eventually arrived at the beach, which was a relatively rare phenomenon, my friend and I were expected to walk casually back along the short jetty to where the interested onlookers were standing, beam up at them from our innocent, eleven year old faces, and ask them if they would like a trip around Portland Harbour. Sometimes it worked and sometimes it didn't.

Our evenings on the boat would begin at about 6.30 and end around 9 o'clock, providing we didn't get any late customers, in which case we would make their twenty minute trip the last one of the evening. On our way home, Brian, who was the official boat handler, would very often give my friend and me a couple of shillings each for our trouble, or, if it was a particularly warm evening, he would buy us a bottle of cold Pepsi from the drinks machine that was situated at the side of the post office in Castletown. This might not sound like much of a reward for the time we spent on the boat, but it was actually quite generous of eighteen-year-old Brian, who was paid a third of the total take for the evening, which I remember thinking at the time often amounted to very little and sometimes nothing at all. Looking back on it, I don't think any of us cared too much about what we were being paid. We felt that having the run of the boat for the evening, with the occasional bonus of a trip around the warships, seemed reward enough.

Of all the many evenings I spent on the boat, there is one in particular that stands out in my recollection due to the strong emotions of embarssment and fear, which Brian, Robin and I had to endure at the hands of an outraged Wilkie, who evidently thought he was about to lose the bigger of his two boats, along with his livelihood.

We three comrades were gathered in the smaller boat as usual, when Wilkie unexpectedly returned in the big boat from a deep sea fishing trip with half a dozen anglers on board. Everything went smoothly enough for a while; Wilkie moored his bigger boat alongside our smaller one, the anglers duly departed in good spirits and Wilkie thanked the three of us for helping with the mooring procedure. Then a decision was made that was to change the shape of the otherwise well-rounded and genial atmosphere that had evolved on that pleasant summer's evening by the calm waters of Portland Harbour. Wilkie decided, probably because he was in a good mood from having had a successful day's fishing with his customers (who had all gone home happy) to encourage Brian to untie the big boat from the side of the smaller one, and to have a go at re-mooring it alongside the big stone pier that jutted out into the sea a few feet away from his wooden jetty. This would then allow the small boat to put to sea should anyone require a trip around the harbour. I seem to remember Brian showing some doubt about the wisdom involved in letting him 'have a go' with the bigger boat, but having been under Wilkie's jubilant and generous persuasion for a minute or so, he finally agreed to try his skill.

He jumped into the little wheelhouse, after the restraining ropes had been released, and with Wilkie shouting directions from the stone pier, proceeded to throttle up the engine in order to get away from the wooden jetty. Robin and I were on the deck of the bigger boat and could see at first hand the nervous look on Brian's face, as the stern of the boat began to drift in the wrong direction. With his hands spinning themselves into a blur on the wheel, Brian stared out through the front of the wheelhouse window with a look of strained concentration that seemed to enlarge the whites of his eyes until they appeared almost to light up the dark interior of the housing in which he was stood.

Having been told several times by an already visibly irate Wilkie to, "Get the arse of it round," Brian began to gain some kind of control over the direction of the boat, and we found ourselves pointing bow first towards the side of the solid stone pier and about twenty feet away from it.

Now came the tricky bit. Brian had next to increase the speed of the engine by just the right amount, in order to bring the craft into the pier until the bow was virtually touching the stonework, at which time he would have to throttle right down so that the bow would gently touch against the pier. He would then need to turn the wheel until the rudder was in the correct position to cause the boat to swing in sideways, thereby completing the manouvre and leaving us snugly alongside the pier, when ropes would be thrown to Wilkie, who would secure us fore and aft. The reason for this complex manouvering was due to the fact that the larger boat was somewhat hemmed in between the stone pier, the wooden jetty and some stanchions that supported an extension to the pier. However, its usual mooring position was at the center of this triangle, and as we all knew, Wilkie never had a problem with the manouvering, which seemed to suggest that a practiced boat handler such as Brian wouldn't either, especially with Wilkie issuing instructions from the nearby pier.

Well, the reason why this event has stayed so vividly in my mind for the last forty years, is quite simply because from then on circumstances were to arise, which would not only test the stress levels of the boat, but also of the four people involved in the endeavour as well. I believe I'm right in saying that Brian made a couple of dodgy runs at the wall, which proved to be too slow. After we'd floated around in a semi-circle for a minute after each attempt, he then decided to come at the pier a little faster, so that we would actually make contact. Now, anyone who has handled a boat, or who has watched one being handled, will know that when you reduce the speed of the engine, in order to slow the vessel down, a fair-sized boat such as Wilkie's doesn't come to a dead stop. You either have to let it drift to a standstill, which often results in the boat moving forwards for several feet, depending on how fast you're traveling in the first place, or you put the whole thing in reverse, which brings you to a stop considerably more quickly, but if overdone can cause you to end up going backwards and away from your destination. On this occasion, however, we drifted forwards far too quickly and made a shuddering contact with the solid Portland stone out of which the pier was constructed. And all this after Wilkie had been screaming at Brian to slow the bugger down.

The cracking sound that emanated from the timbers of the boat as we struck home made me wince as though I was in physical pain. Robin stood looking aghast with a coil of rope in his hands, in readiness for throwing onto the pier at Wilkie's feet, while Wilkie busied himself by snatching the oily cloth cap from his head, which he then threw to the ground. Scarlet faced, he proceeded to jump up and down on it, while yelling incoherent sounds at poor Brian, whose hands had again become a blur upon the steering wheel. To make matters worse, the boat seemed to lodge itself at an odd angle against the pier and nothing Brian could do would shift it. There was nothing Wilkie could do to help because the top of the stone pier where he was standing was several feet above the side of the boat, and he wasn't able to reach down far enough to be able to fend us away with his hands.

Fortunately, Brian had a brainwave. He grabbed a wooden pole that was lying on deck, and having previously shut down the speed of the engine, rushed forwards with his pole to fend us away from the stonework. All went well for a few seconds, until he clumsily dropped the pole into the sea, where it floated just out of reach. For some inexplicable reason my eleven-year-old mind found his red-faced exertions, as he leant over the side desperately straining towards the pole, exceedingly funny. As Wilkie began a fresh wave of ranting above us, I (much to my embarassment and shame) became unexplainably seized by a bout of giggling, which soon developed into screams of laughter that doubled me over. I seem to remember feeling frightened that I couldn't stop my raucous gaffawing, especially when Brian turned to me and started swearing in my direction.

To cut an already over-long story short, Brian somehow managed to retrieve the pole, even without my help, and the heated moment soon calmed down, as the boat was at last brought safely up against the side of the pier and tied up. My memory of what was said after that is very blurred, but I think that when Wilkie realised that no permanent damage had been done the conversation returned to a more normal tone, and I do remember timidly apologising to Brian as we walked home. He was surprisingly good humoured about the fact that I seemed to find his plight hysterically funny, perhaps realising that it was probably a reaction to my own nervous state.

MOVEMENT

A new beginning for winter's aggression is marked by the gale beating out its warning of increasing movement through a loose cable on the telegraph pole.

My eyes protest, as they look into the blur that is the sea. All my senses vibrate in tune with the quickening.

I taste brine on my tongue and smell it in the air, as in a panic I gasp breath into my lungs when the rushing wind appears to be trying to smother me. A million pebbles move to assault my ears. My skin feels cold and lashed, as I lean my body against the new master.

An army of serpent-like waves with forces unknown and unimaginable make clear the threat, whipped up by the once weightless and impotent dictator, they display their anger through tops of foaming froth - a sample of their venom spat high above the rattling hordes rains down.

A fury in a grey and colourless domain soon forces my retreat back down the hill to sanity.

I glance back up at the bedlam that dances on the sea wall and note the increasing stream of venom running down the hill. The full attack is yet to come, but the flooding of hearts and minds is a sudden and unforeseen destiny. This feast of vengeance is set to write its memoirs in the homes of those who sought to share their lives as neighbours to the tranquil side of movement's schizophrenic nature.

From the safety of the opposing hill I watch, as movement's forces gather in a deepening swirl around the doorways of unprotected cottages that lie at the bottom. Even though the attack will last but a few short hours, its passion will live on in the memories of those who dwell within, as the symbols of their hearts become ravaged and ruined before their eyes: furniture, carpets and wall paper - all seemingly mundane, yet chosen by the heart in order to display its love become warped and tarnished by the violent surge.

At last a slower time returns. Reports from the aftermath talk of burdens bravely borne and shared - of relationships renewed and strengthened. A sense of unity and comradeship prevails, as though to balance that which seemed to be created of only destruction.

My Royal Manor

A comfortable crown of soft, white vapour adorns the head of the Royal Manor, as I drive towards it on a ribbon of road that runs parallel to Chesil Beach. The beach is nature's monument to its own power, and appears to have been laid out by the encircling sea as a permanent reminder to the little island that it will, one day, succumb to the sea's relentless gnawing and be finally devoured. On this particular day, the ocean reflects the calm of a blue sky and a joyous sun, as I drive up the hill towards the vaporous crown, where eternal threats have no place on a day that seems so full of promise.

Within a minute, I have passed through the crown and find myself on a cloudless summer trail that heads towards Portland Bill. Stone is the theme of the landscape on this trail; where once small, green, rolling hills gave tranquil pasture to sheep, a dismembering force has ripped and blown the maternal scene into wasted valleys. And yet, through man's need for shelter, nature has formed a unique character in this place that people now fear to lose.

Within another minute, I have passed the stony landmark of St. Georges Church and have left the scars of violent change behind. I travel down sloping green, past the Royal Manor College, where once the playing field added to the emerald effect, but now is overgrown with structures designed to further the human appreciation of life. My escapade through tiny Portland advances so quickly that the approaching village is soon behind me, whereupon an expanse to my left affects me with a fresh revelation of old land wounds, which lie unhealed in Portland's yielding heart.

In but a dozen breaths, I have passed another village, and now before me lies the final slope that ends at Portland Bill, where the stern of the Royal Manor dips like a sinking ship into the sea - the point marked by a lighthouse, which seems to say, "Take care! For once upon the rocks, you too will slip away."

In five short minutes, I have travelled the length of this often overlooked island. I park my car and stand alone at the water's edge, watching the eternity of movement displayed therein. There are dozens of people enjoying the beautiful effect of contrast between land and water on this summer's day, though not the thousands there might have been, had the sea conspired with the land to give birth to a sandy beach, rather than Chesil's rattling, rolling pile.

I take a short stroll to the pub, where I stand with my pint, looking through the window at the thinly scattered, small groups of people who are still walking near the water's edge. As I calmly sip on my beer, I notice the dance of the sunlight at a place on the ever-moving surface of the sea that seems almost to wink at me. I smile when it occurs to me that the kingdom of the Royal Manor, although small and in places roughly hewn, is a kingdom rare among the places of the modern world. Then I raise my glass towards the scene behind the window, and in a moment of supreme selfishness, I return the wink that I received from the dancing sunlight, and raising a toast to the island's health, I say, "And long may you stay overlooked!"

'OUT THE WEARES'

A feeling came to me, as I sat quite recently, visualising dreams of long ago.

Is it really forty years since I shouted, 'Out the Weares!' after Mother said she'd really like to know,

Where were we going to? and what we planned to do? as dinner would be in an hour, or so.

An hour is forever when you're doing something clever, like climbing trees and hanging from a bough.

Just staring in a pond seemed so exciting then, but alas! it doesn't seem so now.

Throwing pebbles in the sea when it was nearly time for tea, caused more annoyance to poor Mum and Dad;

With shoes all salty white we must have looked a sight, but appearances could never make us sad.

The fogey up the road, looking out from his abode, used to shout at us when we were playing ball.

He didn't understand that there was nothing underhand - we'd only made a goal against his wall.

Cheeky though we were and though wrath we did incur, there was never harm in anything we did.

Laughing, shouting, jumping, the worst we did was scrumping - belly-ache to an unwary kid!

After all is said and done, growing older - where's the fun? There's none for us, it sometimes seems to be.

But look across at Chesil and you'll still see little devils, as they laugh and throw big pebbles in the sea.

So, if you're old and grey and kids get in your way, stop and think of all the fun that *you* once had.

Relive it for a day and just watch the kids at play, and - just maybe - life won't seem quite so bad.

PORTLAND AND ME

Standing alone I gaze out to sea - I'm at Portland Heights, where Yeates used to be.
Remember the sixties when I was a boy - from here my old school looks just like a toy.
The harbour's expanse so graceful and blue, once captured on photo's I took for the view.
The houses where I grew up as a lad - so many good memories and very few bad.
Turn to the south and St. Georges looms clear, my ancestors rest in the graveyard just here.
This island which once gave birth to this soul, which shaped all my memories, which makes me feel whole, which nourished and raised so many who've gone, which nourishes still the ones who live on.

Unique in your landscape, unique in your past - preserve in my heart the die that you've cast.

And when at last I'm saying goodbye, to this island of stone - it will not be a lie to say that my lot has been of the best, as on this noble island I'm laid to my rest.

For though we are modern and sometimes feel scorn, and turn our backs on the place where we're born -

Still we come back to the place in our hearts - the place we call home, where our childhood starts.

Portland and the Sunset Dream

With the jagged silhouette of Portland's West Weare cliffs to the left of us, and the mighty, rolling shoulder of Chesil beach sweeping a curve to the right, we gaze straight ahead from our position on Portland's sea wall, across the enormous expanse of water that is West Bay. The sound of the small, gently lapping waves upon the pebbles below the sea wall make a gentle ripple in our otherwise becalmed senses. The summer air is heavy and still, as the lights in nature's huge theatre begin to very slowly dim in a dramatic build up to sunset, which is the main event in this production.

It occurs to me that sunset is a reflection of our own being: the deep blue verging nearly to black, sprinkled with stars like pinpoints of hope, the increasing brilliance of wonder, and finally the orange explosion of recreation at the center.

We stand, cameras in hand, waiting for the prime moment, when the contrast of colour is at its peak, before the button is pressed and the magic becomes trapped - encoded digitally inside the oblong box, where no real image could ever be contained.

We arrive home and, first things first - we make some tea. The tea ritual is followed by the connection process - small, oblong box to large, oblong box. Two more buttons are pressed and our sunset dream is reborn upon the screen, the image as real as the original, but smaller. The encoding merely hid the dream from us for the duration of the journey home. "Thank God!" we cry, "The dream never really died at all." We sit and look at our Chesil sunset, which now will last forever.

Sometime later, I sit and reflect upon our visit to Chesil Beach, and an image of the sunset that we witnessed comes into my mind, where no real image could ever be contained.

Portland Castle

Gleaming white, the fortress stands enhanced in light by summer's heartening glow. The monument to war-like dreams, immovable and built from fear, looks out across the moving blue towards a harbour view that's clear of smoke and dust and death, the hellish sound of canon's breath and other torments far beyond the scope of words to show.

A piece of Portland, hewn and shaped to suit a king, whose counterpart of similar heart sought to bring the ravages and suffering of war to Portland's shore. But for the turn of fate the harbour's calm serenity might have held a memory of battles long ago. The changing shape of history allows us now to view the castle's presence with relief - a reminder of a time of folly, shaped by ignorance, desire and belief.

Today within the castle, enactments of a play inspired by the past are filled with humorous quality, enjoyed through known security and calmness of the mind. The canon's crash is now a thrill, designed to make our children laugh in opposition to the ancient theme; for then the plan was pain and death, children left bereft of fathers, whose final statement would have been a scream.

To walk among the battlements and out upon the green is a joy for those who know that freedom means a life without the threat of war. Perhaps we've learned to live beyond the endless cries for more, and will forever keep at bay the canon's roar.

PORTLAND'S EASTERN SIDE

I once took a photograph of Portland's eastern side and thought I would explode with pride at such a view; for running down along the cliff from Grove to Bill was vibrant colour left and right (the blue and green is with me still) divided by a plunging line of grey, all basking 'neath a brilliant sun upon that glowing August day. The solid rocks - too hard for flesh to penetrate - contrast with air too rare to feel, as through it drifts a single gull - experience born on the wind that fascinates and holds me in its free and floating state.

I trudge ahead towards the distant red and white of Portland's famous warning light, and glancing down to where the railway ran I find nostalgia's subtle hand draughted up to meet me, as though upon a rush of steam projected from the past. To think that once I yearned to be away from beauty such as this - a young man drawn towards a city's window-dressing lure, where variety and complication mean the same - a fact that lies concealed through youthful inexperience, which state of mind is best described as bliss.

But now perspective changes course and clears the lens, allowing photographic therapy to help me mend my broken dream of Portland. For if I live to be infirm and cannot make the walk to Portland's eastern side, perhaps I will, with pride, be able still to show a photo' of its charms - a

Portland's Farewell

A rumbling sound around the bay that shook and throbbed throughout the day set Weymouth people wondering just what the cause of such a quake could be. Windows cracked as houses shook; people hid, afraid to look for fear of the destruction they might see.

"Portland's on the move!" said one. "Her anchor is a mile long, we've seen it dragged up 'side the cliffs. She's going now - drifting off beneath a setting sun."

'Twas true the island's mind was set on leaving, her ancient place dissolving through a dream of solitude that, at the risk of seeming rude, Portland would pursue until the end.

She drifted north past glaciers and wilderness, minus those who'd cut her bits away - they didn't stay, they left her in their frightened droves without a friend - that is except for one, an ageing gent whose hearing aid he sought to mend, for who but someone deaf could fail to hear the call to up and run?

The borough's Mare became involved on learning of the island's loss, and showed concern when looking at the cost of such a rumpus.

"This means that my official name is 'Mayor of Weymouth And' - it's not the same without the Portland bit," she said, and asked advice from councillors who thought that what was needed was a compass.

A boat despatched to do the search went south instead of north, the crew assuming islands always head for warmer climes. But Portland now was miles away, exploring lonely coasts and knowing colder times.

The deaf old gent, the truth to tell, was also glad to be alone, and settled down to hibernate with ample fuel to burn and food upon his plate he'd taken from the shops. He'd eaten well of Christmas cake and lollipops then gone to bed in overcoats, scarves, gloves and woolly hats he'd jammed upon his head.

The coast of Greenland now in sight enticed the little island with the solitude she craved. She settled in along a stretch where icy cliffs embraced her mood, and moaning winds were all that could be heard. Of people there were none and even polar bears were rare, which saved her from the company of kimberlins and other folk, who'd mostly cut her innards out and spread the pieces all about - oh yes, they'd had their share of Portland's yolk. But now what would they do? She'd drifted off and taken all their stone. Soon they'd have nowhere to live, which served them right! They'd only ever used her, now she'd rather be alone.

Days passed by. The old man died, peacefully beneath a pile of blankets. Now the sound of snoring was no more and Portland rested, silent as the grave. A year went by and then some more - how long would she wait there for? A billion years to make the move, to rush off now was not what she intended.

The island slumbered, made drowsy by the moaning wind that hummed a lullaby; then unexpectedly awakened, as cold began to crack her skin, which let the damp come streaming in. Expansion pushed the fissures wide 'till water ran down deep inside and cracked the stone - the fabric of her soul.

Now wide-awake, little Portland panicked. She'd dreamt of when she used to be surrounded by a warmer sea. Oh! How the shock was felt; enough to make an iceberg melt - the startled heat from Portland's agitation. Her stone all cracked and split away, she could not stay there one more day, attacked by freezing cold and condensation. Being loathed to bear a grudge and filled with thoughts of yesterday, she knew the time to move away had come. And so the homeward trudge began through freezing fog.

She passed Iceland where geezers blew their tops. Surprised to see her floating through they gave their spouts an extra blast - their previous goodbyes they still remembered, for surely only recently they'd gushed farewell, as Portland passed the other way, saying as she went, "Goodbye forever!" "Well," they said, "Perhaps a week had gone, but nothing more" - a geezer's guess at time was never clever.

At last she floated gently back, up to the coast of Dorset - her original domain. A starlit sky exposed her silhouette. A mile out from Weymouth Bay she slowed right down, almost to a stop, and there she had a bet. She wagered she could slip back in before the dawn and carry on just as before, with any luck no-one would notice she was there. She breathed a sigh and drifted in to Chesil Beach, the pebbles now within her reach rustled gently, as she bedded in. Then, when the sun arose illuminating all around, Portland could be seen again, as though she'd never gone,

Quarrying

The solid heart of stone that supports its children is cut out by ceaseless toil amid sweat and pain. To know life's beauty is to fear its loss, which gives rise to survival's river of need. The river is a torrent that hammers, slices and drills the white mass into a shape that shelters those that feel the fullness of the flowing tide. To repeat the dismembering action through a lifetime is the price that becomes tolled out by the sound of metal on stone. The stone is turned by effort and struggle into an edifice of beauty. The transference of pain into pleasure appears complete and seems to be an end in itself. But who will tend and care for the edifice? Eternity endlessly borrows from itself then looks on.

Quarrying (version 2)

Heaving the weight to crack up the stone. Metal on metal, the grunt and the groan. Year after year amid toil and sweat, cutting and splitting the stone that is set into ground as unyielding as wanting and need. The rent to be paid and six mouths to feed. The quarryman's lot a fifty-year stretch to fetch and to carry the bits of his homeland that others require, in order to show off their dreams of desire;

Stating their power through carvings of white and buildings of splendour that indicate might, and the force that is needed to keep into place the level of wealth that some people need to satisfy greed. How long will it be 'till the tyranny ends?

It ends when we think of each other as friends.

THE FISHERMAN

With brown skin like tarred rope, and a shining smile that compliments the patch of reflected sunlight on his bald head, the fisherman slams his Wellington boots into the sloping, shifting rock pile that is Chesil Beach, as he strides to his working day. He drags his small, wooden rowing dinghy down to the curling water's edge, where the sea is fussily washing and re-washing the shoreline pebbles that seem to have found themselves within its care.

Once afloat, the fisherman begins to row his craft against the incoming waves in a straining battle that the little boat seems barely able to win. A few yards farther out and he stops rowing, in order to shout at someone who is stood upon the sea wall, gazing out under a cupped hand that shields squinting eyes from the dancing, thrusting light being reflected by the summer blue.

"Tell Comben I'll be back in time for him to buy me a pint at the Cove Inn!" laughs the fisherman, while with practised strokes he heaves the dinghy onwards against the weight of nature's movement, towards a row of bobbing, orange-coloured marker buoys.

On arriving at the place where expectancy meets the hidden truth of possible reward, weathered hands work quickly to pull the lobster pots to the surface. Disappointment registers briefly in the blue eyes, as the last uninhabited pot is thrown back into the depths of the ocean's constantly changing lottery. A white smile quickly resumes its usual place at the centre of the brown face of our champion of the now, as he heads back to the beach where movement is but a reflection of the ocean's gyrating possibilities.

Upon the fisherman's arrival, the genial atmosphere of the pub expands with the presence of one who has mastered himself.

THE 'I' OF THE BEHOLDER

"Those cliffs look grand," I said to a man, who stood next to me on a beach by the sea.

"They're not grand to me," he replied looking down. "That's where my boy died, at the edge of the tide."

"The sea looks so blue and lovely to me," I said, as I smiled, encouragingly.

"The sea holds my soul," he said, staring out at the blue that trapped him within, as it rolled.

"How long have you lived on Portland?" I asked.

"I don't know, but soon I'll be gone - I can't carry on here. You see it through gloss - this island of stone," he replied in a sad and far-away tone.

"It's a perfect day - not too hot or too cold," I announced with a relish, as a pebble I bowled splashed into the sea - the droplets of spray reflecting to me the joy that I felt at that moment in time - a moment sublime.

"I feel a bit cold," said the man, as he turned and trudged on his way, each step born of burden, he walked as if clay were holding him down - his affect on my mind producing a frown, which vanished as I reclaimed my past, by way of a memory that seemed to last from my time spent on Portland: blackberry bushes and ponds full of frogs, fishermen's nets and weathered old dogs shaking the spray of the sea from their coats, while children laugh as they climb into boats that promise such fun, as we bob on the waves in the heat of the sun.

These memories to me are the Portland I see, as I take a stroll through my mind. But they don't agree with the sad memory of the man with the pain, who carries the thoughts of a boy who was slain. He cannot know the Portland I know with a mind that is free. When I look at this place, is it Portland I see, or is it just me?

The Pond

The pond - a place of excitement to a boy of ten. Feet shod with school shoes, gingerly placed in mud at the water's edge, just close enough to allow the watery risk to lap at the toe cap. In this position, I can almost reach a wavering hand into the slimy, and slightly frightening, clump of weed containing the string of jelly with the black bits in it that the frogs have left behind. The fear of damaging the shoes is finally overcome by the desperate need to possess the jelly. Bent nearly double, I place a foot forward into the water, grab a handful of spawn and lurch backwards triumphant, holding the slippery prize aloft. There ensues a gratifying cheer from my two friends, who are stood at the side of the bomb crater, which the bomb, in its failure to land on target and to maim and kill, once created. The crater has since allowed the formation of the wondrous pond on the common land above Portland's dockyard.

The history of the pond is irrelevant to me, as I am now a bag of mixed emotions. I have gained a handful of spawn, but my shoes are wet and muddy. Last week they each displayed a salt mark from being stampeded too close to the sea at Chesil, where a guilty ocean presented me with the irresistible challenge of trying to outrun its waves, as they crashed up onto the beach. My parents had not been amused. Could the glorious admiration of my friends on this occasion outweigh the fear of possible punishment? I was fraught!

I climb out of the crater and gaze down at the mud on my shoes. I laugh nervously, while pretending to be unperturbed, as my 'friends' point at the mud-splattered source of my future pain, and while laughing and pointing like clowns in a circus, keep repeating, "Look at your shoes!"

The feeling of hero-like supremacy that arose at the sound of their cheers withdraws itself from me, as though it is being sucked out by an enormous syringe. For a second I feel close to tears, as the realisation of my comrades' duplicity sinks in. However, I quickly force a recovery and proceed to put on an act of bravado, which includes walking around, while kicking my feet out. The resultant spray of mud and water that flies off the end of my wet and slimy footwear causes considerable mirth to erupt from my devious colleagues, who laugh heartily for a few seconds. This outburst of pleasure is soon overtaken by a wave of concern, as the two boys look down at the mud splashes on their school trousers and replace their smiles and laughter with frowns and cries of objection. The turn around in events allows me at least some compensation, and I go off with my previously shattered mood somewhat repaired, in search of a clump of grass to wipe my swamp-spoiled shoes on.

Having only succeeded in smearing the mud over an even wider area of my shoes, I give up on my attempt to improve the situation and suggest to my mates, who are spitting on their hands and wiping the now freshly moistened mud over a wide area of their trousers, that we could race each other the hundred or so yards to the next pond, which is bigger than this one and which, I assure them, contains bigger frogs and more spawn than the hopeless pond we've been wasting our time at.

We dash off in the direction of the next bomb crater yelling, "Frogs!" at the top of our voices. When we arrive at the edge of the water-filled crater, I notice that it has an almost identical piece of rusty pipe sticking up out of the water to the piece of pipe that was sticking out of the other pond. I'd noticed this phenomenon in other ponds on other parts of the island, and I wonder for a moment where all the pieces of pipe might be coming from.

We are about to embark on a similar round of risk taking with my friend Steve now assuming the role of spawn collector, when I feel two or three large spots of rain land on my head, followed swiftly by dozens more. We look at one another with resigned expressions for a few seconds, until Steve, who is now standing with his feet gingerly placed in mud at the water's edge, takes a step back onto firmer soil and announces that we have been out for hours and that we should have gone straight home from school. The increasing velocity of the raindrops that are bouncing off of my head seem to underline the truth of his statement. None of us is wearing a watch, but Mark, who is the other member of our trio, takes the initiative by waving his hand above his head as though he is leading a cavalry charge, and with a worried look on his face shouts, "Quick! We've got to get home!"

THE VAPOUR SHROUD

A landscape that is closed down by fog presents a smaller world. Misty, white silence surrounds the cold nuggets of stone that lie scattered on the floor of the gouge that is the quarry. Silence gives way to the vibration of heavy boots tramping over hard ruts of dried earth. The sound announces the dark figure before it evolves through the white, where it reveals itself to be an old man in a black overcoat. He plods along in weary fashion, looking neither left or right. Behind him a black dog emerges from the deep, lacy curtain. Unlike the old man, the young dog's enthusiasm moves him from side to side - the probing, sniffing nose momentarily ruling the all but lifeless scene. The pair continue through the barren space until their shrouded exit allows the sleep of stillness, where the need to know expires, to resume its effortless dominance of the empty quarry.

The old man and his companion trudge on towards a home built of the cold, sleeping stone through which they have just passed. On entering the house a fire is lit. The warmth radiates throughout the stonework, but fails to comfort the old man, who seems to have retained the emptiness of the quarry within his heart. With tail wagging the dog lies by the fire, while his master sits in a well-worn chair by the hearth and stares vacantly at the empty chair opposite, looking for his life's lost reflection.

A day has passed and an optimistic sun burns away the quarry's misty shroud. The old man and his companion have chosen to walk a different route, where passers-by greet their elevated mood with equal cheer upon a sunny, bustling pavement. The quarry too has visitors - some birds upon a slab of stone look on as butterflies flit through the quarry's shimmering haze.

Far out to sea a white mist gathers, shepherded by tomorrow's breeze.

Whose Boy Is It?

"Whose boy is it?" The question was asked by an old Portlander who was sitting on a dry-stone wall watching a young man, who was running past with a sandwich tin under his arm and a worried look on his face.

"You wanna get up in the morning, me son." The advice on early rising followed the unanswered question regarding his identity, as the young man ran on towards a pile of white, stone blocks that were built up near to the entrance of the quarry he was heading for.

The old man turned to his companion - another aged Portlander, who was sat to the left of the first, his legs crossed in a casual manner, while his right thumb and forefinger clasped at the base of a piece of straw. The other end of the straw was held lightly between the old fellow's teeth, in order that it could be 'twizzled' back and forth. This particular gentleman was shaking his head in the resigned way the older generation reserves for the antics of the young. His gaze followed the running figure of the quarryman, as in the summer sun the lad's boots kicked up little puffs of stone dust.

"That's young Pearce, innit?" The head shaker suddenly felt it was important to verify the identity of the running, late arrival.

"Think so. Good job 'is father's the foreman. In my day they'd 'ave docked 'is wages."

The two men continued to watch, as the figure disappeared into a stone-cutting shed.

"Time was," continued the first, "When stone on this island 'ad a future. Not any more."

"Not any more," echoed the second old-timer, throwing his piece of straw down in disgust. "Nineteen sixty, and who would 'ave thought things would turn out like they are, Harry, eh?"

"I dunno," replied Harry, who was at that precise moment considering giving up offering advice to young men on their way to work. He leaned forward from his seat on the wall and adjusted his trouser turn-ups in a way that better suited his mood. He glanced briefly at his 'old men's boots'- a name given to his footwear by his grandson, who as a child had seemed to find fascination in playing with the many lace holes that ran up past the ankle. He noticed a certain amount of stone dust had alighted on the toe caps, which increased the mild agitation he was already feeling.

"We got skiffle groups now, Joseph. 'Ave you 'eard any of 'em?"

Joseph sat with his hands on his knees and blew out his cheeks. Having exhaled some of his own dissatisfaction with life, he merely replied, "No, I 'aven't."

"I was tryin' to 'ave a quiet cup of tea in thik café up the road the other day," continued Harry, "And the noise comin' out of that thing in the corner - jukebox I think they call it. Rock 'n' Roll - more like thunder 'n' lightnin'."

Joseph clapped his hands on the knees they'd been previously clasping and declared it was time to move on, as the missus would be, "Wantin' some 'elp in a minute."

With caps freshly adjusted, the two father's of leisure proceeded gently up the road under an increasingly hot sun, doing up their jackets as they went - the modern penchant for stripping off in the summer heat being considered unwise and a luxury that would, 'Bring about its own reprisals in the end'.

Printed in Great Britain
by Amazon

74891916R00037